This Ladybird Book belongs to:

Lynsey Kirk

Ladybird

*This Ladybird retelling
by
Audrey Daly*

Ladybird books are widely available, but in case of
difficulty may be ordered by post or telephone from:

Ladybird Books – Cash Sales Department
Littlegate Road Paignton Devon TQ3 3BE
Telephone 0803 554761

A catalogue record for this book is available
from the British Library

First edition

Published by Ladybird Books Ltd Loughborough Leicestershire UK
Ladybird Books Inc Auburn Maine 04210 USA

Printed in England

FAVOURITE TALES

The Little Mermaid

illustrated
by
BRIAN PRICE THOMAS

based on the story by Hans Christian Andersen

Wherever the wide sky arches above them and soft breezes blow, people have always made their homes. They live on mountains, in deserts, and beside the sea.

But once, long ago, there were people who lived *under* the sea. The King of the mer-people had his palace in the very deepest part of the ocean. There he lived with his six pretty daughters.

The Princesses were too young to visit the world above the sea, but the youngest one never tired of hearing her grandmother talk of it.

Sometimes at night, as the youngest Princess gazed up through the cool, clear water, a shadow would pass overhead.

The little mermaid knew that it was a ship, full of strange creatures who had legs instead of the tails that all mer-people had.

One day the oldest Princess was allowed to rise to the surface. On her return, she told of the cities she had seen and the music she had heard. She told of the sound of bells and the perfume of flowers.

The little mermaid listened, and yearned for the day when it would be her turn to visit the world above.

When at last the youngest Princess was allowed to go to the surface, she looked around in wonder. Close by was a ship. She could see the people inside enjoying a birthday party, given for the Prince who was on board.

Then, very suddenly, a storm blew up.
The wind was so strong that it turned
the ship over. The waves beat against
the ship, breaking it to pieces.

The little mermaid saw the Prince in
the water. He had almost drowned,
and he was too weak to swim. Swiftly,
she came to his rescue.

When the storm ended, the little mermaid took the Prince to the shore and left him lying in the sunshine. He was very pale and still, and his eyes were closed.

Then the little mermaid swam out to sea and waited to see what would happen. Before long some young girls found the Prince.

At first the girls thought the Prince was dead. But he soon opened his eyes and sat up.

The little mermaid watched, and her heart filled with sadness. The Prince would never know that she was the one who had rescued him. Slowly, she swam home to her father's palace.

When her sisters asked what she had seen, the little mermaid told them only of a ship and the seashore.

But in the days that followed, she often swam to where she had left the Prince, hoping she might see him again. She never did.

The little mermaid was so sad that at last she told her sisters what had happened.

"I know the palace where the Prince lives!" said one of her sisters. "I'll take you to see it."

After that, the little mermaid swam to the palace nearly every day, longing for even a glimpse of the Prince. She had fallen in love with him.

The little mermaid talked with her grandmother about the world of humans. "Do men live for ever if they are not drowned?" she asked.

"No," replied her grandmother. "They die just as we do. But when we die, we just become foam on the sea. Humans have souls, and when they die their souls go to a wonderful place far away."

"Is there any way I could get a soul?" asked the little mermaid.

"Only if a human falls in love with you," said her grandmother. "And humans prefer people with legs."

This made the little mermaid sadder than ever. "There must be *something* I can do," she thought to herself.

In desperation, the little mermaid decided to visit a witch. The journey was terrifying, and several times she nearly turned back. But thoughts of the Prince gave her courage, and at last she came to the witch's house.

"So you want legs?" hissed the witch. "Very well. But losing your tail will be terribly painful. And if the Prince marries someone else, you will become foam on the sea."

"I still want to try," said the little mermaid.

"One thing more," said the witch. "You must give me your voice as payment."

The little mermaid agreed. She loved the Prince so much that she would have agreed to anything.

So the witch gave her a magic potion to drink. From the moment she took it, the little mermaid would be dumb.

The little mermaid swam to the Prince's palace and drank the potion. She felt a sharp pain, then fell into a deep sleep. When she awoke, her gleaming tail had gone. She had legs like a human girl.

When the Prince saw the beautiful
stranger, he asked her who she was.
She could only smile in reply.

The little mermaid was so lovely that
the Prince gave her beautiful clothes
to wear and took her with him wherever
he went.

One evening there was a party at the
palace. All the guests admired the silent
mysterious girl who danced as gracefully
as the waves of the sea.

As time went by, the Prince grew more and more fond of the little mermaid. But he did not ask her to marry him.

One day he told her he was going to another country. "I am going to meet a princess there," he explained. "My parents hope I will marry her. But I know I will not love her. I love another girl," the Prince went on. "She once saved me from drowning.

But I do not know where she is. You look a little like her, and if I must marry someone else, I would rather marry you."

The little mermaid was sad, for without a voice, she could not tell the Prince the truth.

The Prince took the little mermaid with him on his journey.

When he met the Princess, he was dazzled by her beauty. "You are the girl who saved my life!" he said. And he started to plan their wedding.

The little mermaid thought her heart would break. But there was nothing she could do. The wedding took place, and a big party was held on board the Prince's ship.

That night the little mermaid leaned
over the ship's rail and looked up at
the sky. She knew that when the sun
rose, she would die.

Suddenly the little mermaid's sisters appeared in the water below. They were pale, and all their long hair had gone.

"We gave our hair to the witch in return for a magic knife," they said. "Kill the Prince with it before sunrise, and you will become a mermaid once more."

The little mermaid took the knife and went to where the Prince was sleeping.

But her heart was still full of love,
and she could not kill him.

After taking one last look at the
Prince, she threw herself into the sea.
Slowly, she melted into the foam.

As the sun rose, the little mermaid found herself high in the sky. Glowing lights and sweet voices surrounded her. "Where am I?" she asked.

"With the daughters of the air," said the voices. "We earn our souls by helping anyone who suffers. You can earn a soul too."

Far below, the Prince sailed on with his new bride. They wondered where the little mermaid was.

They did not know that she was high above them, smiling down at them through the sunlit air.

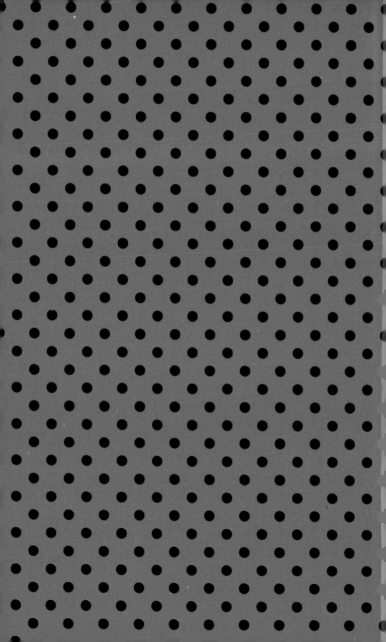